YEARLING BOOKS/YOUNG YEARLINGS/YEARLING CLASSICS are designed especially to entertain and enlighten young people. Patricia Reilly Giff, consultant to this series, received her bachelor's degree from Marymount College and a master's degree in history from St. John's University. She holds a Professional Diploma in Reading and a Doctorate of Humane Letters from Hofstra University. She was a teacher and reading consultant for many years, and is the author of numerous books for young readers.

For a complete listing of all Yearling titles,
write to Dell Readers Service,
P.O. Box 1045, South Holland, IL 60473.

The Pancake

ANITA LOBEL

A Young Yearling Book

Published by
Dell Publishing
a division of
Bantam Doubleday Dell Publishing Group, Inc.
666 Fifth Avenue
New York, New York 10103

The trademark Yearling® is registered in the U.S. Patent and Trademark Office.

The trademark Dell® is registered in the U.S. Patent and Trademark Office.

ISBN: 0-440-40624-2

Reprinted by arrangement with William Morrow & Co., Inc., on behalf of Greenwillow Books

Printed in the United States of America

May 1992

10 9 8 7 6 5 4 3 2 1

WES

Once there was a woman

who had seven hungry children.

She cooked them a pancake.

It lay in the pan

and swelled and rose

and grew thick and tempting.

The children stood

around the stove.

They could not wait

to taste the pancake.

"Please, mother," they cried,

"let us eat the pancake right away!

We are so hungry."

"Wait, my dear ones,"

said the woman.

"Before we eat,

I must flip the pancake over

and cook it on the other side."

When the pancake heard
that it was to be eaten,
it jumped out of the pan
and rolled like a wheel
through the door
and onto the road.

"Wait, wait," cried the woman.
"My children are hungry.
Do not run away from us!"
The woman ran after the pancake
with the pan in one hand
and the spoon in the other.
The seven children ran after her.
"Catch it! Grab it! Hold it!"
the children shouted.
But the pancake rolled faster
and faster down the road.
Soon the woman and the children
were left far behind.

After a while, the pancake met
a farmer. "Good day, farmer,"
said the pancake as it rolled by.
"Good day, pancake," said the farmer.
"You look good enough to eat.
Do not roll away so quickly.
Stop and let me have
a bite out of you!"

"If I can roll away from

the woman who cooked me,

and her seven children

who wanted to eat me,

I can roll away from you too,

dumb farmer," said the pancake.

And off it rolled.

Soon it met a goose.

"Good day, goose," said the pancake.

"Good day, pancake," said the goose.

"You look very delicious.

Do not roll away so quickly.

Stop and let me take

a bite out of you."

"If I can roll away from

the woman who cooked me,

and her seven children

who wanted to eat me,

and a dumb farmer

who wanted to take

a bite out of me,

I can roll away from you too,

silly goose," said the pancake.

And off it rolled.

Soon it met a cat.

"Good day, cat," said the pancake.

"Good day, pancake," said the cat.
"You look very tasty. Do not roll
away so quickly. Stop and let me
take a bite out of you."

"If I can roll away from
the woman who cooked me,
and her seven children
who wanted to eat me,
a dumb farmer
and a silly goose
who wanted to take
a bite out of me,
I can roll away from you too,
stupid cat," said the pancake.
And off it rolled.

The pancake rolled and rolled.

Soon it met a sheep.

"Good day, sheep,"

said the pancake.

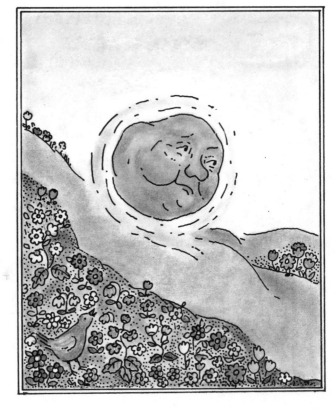

"Good day, pancake," said the sheep.
"You look very sweet. Do not roll
away so quickly. Stop and let me
take a bite out of you."

"If I can roll away from
the woman who cooked me,
and her seven children
who wanted to eat me,
a dumb farmer
and a silly goose
and a stupid cat who wanted
to take a bite out of me,
I can roll away from you too,
foolish sheep," said the pancake.
And off it rolled.

The pancake kept on rolling
down the road.
Soon it met a goat.
"Good day, goat,"
said the pancake.
"Good day, pancake,"
said the goat.
"You look very crunchy.
Do not roll away so quickly.
Stop and let me take a bite
out of you."

"If I can roll away from
the woman who cooked me,
and her seven children
who wanted to eat me,
a dumb farmer
and a silly goose
and a stupid cat
and a foolish sheep
who wanted to take
a bite out of me,
I can roll away from you too,
old goat," said the pancake.
And off it rolled.

The pancake came to a brook.

By the brook stood a pig.

"Good day, pig," said the pancake.

"Good day, pancake," said the pig.

What a mouth-watering pancake,

thought the pig.

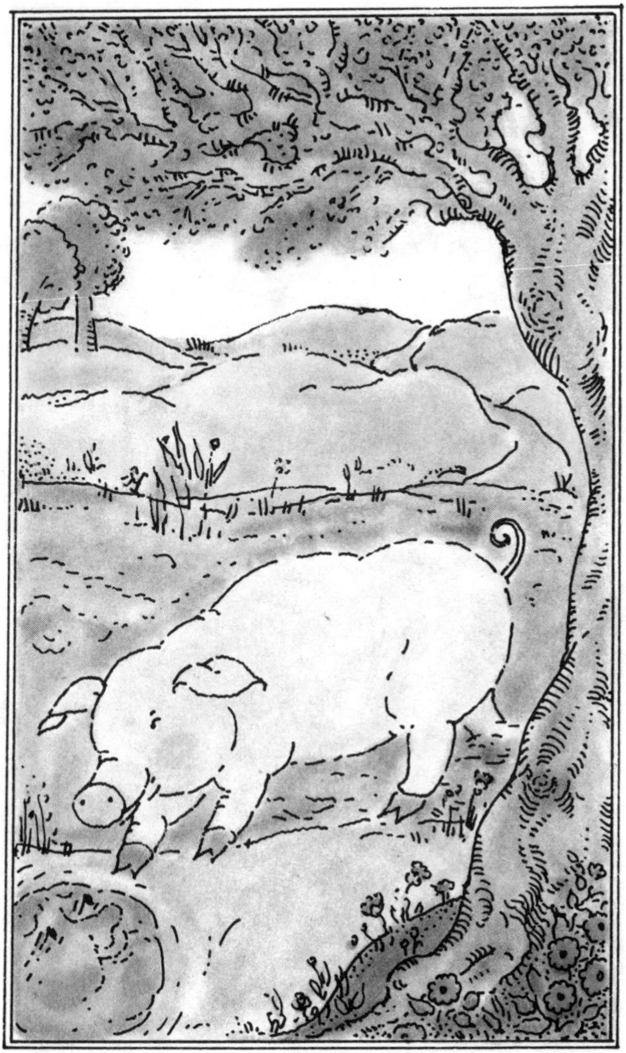

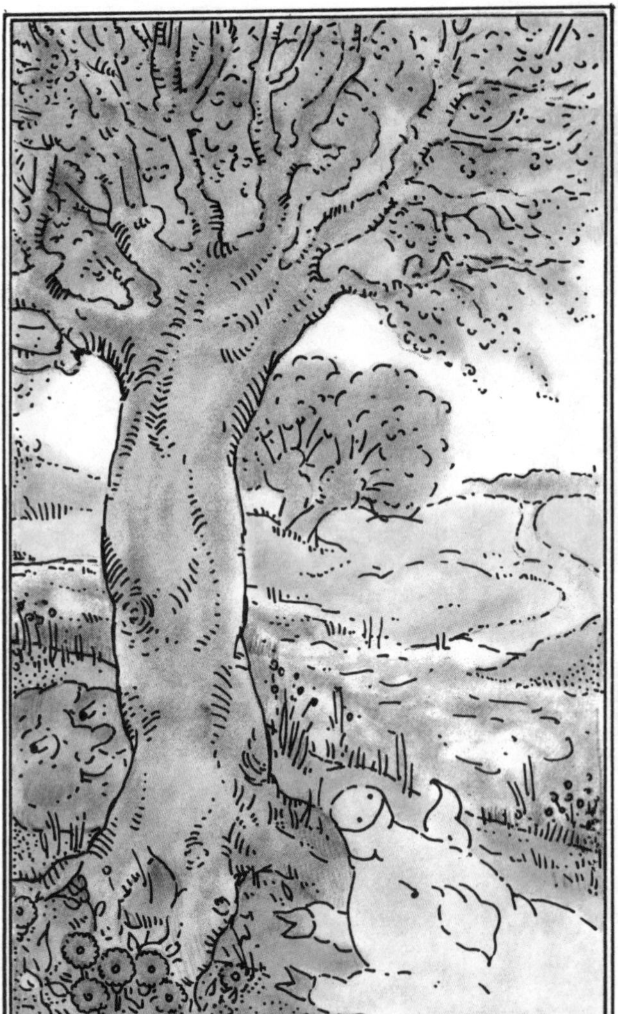

"I have rolled away from

the woman who cooked me,

and her seven children

who wanted to eat me,

a dumb farmer,

a silly goose,

a stupid cat,

a foolish sheep,

and an old goat

who all wanted bites out of me,"

bragged the pancake to the pig.

"I should be able to get across

this brook without becoming

wet and soggy!"

"I will help you," said the pig.

"Just sit on the tip of my nose and
I will take you to the other side."
How clever of me to meet
such a kind pig, thought the pancake
and rolled onto the pig's nose.

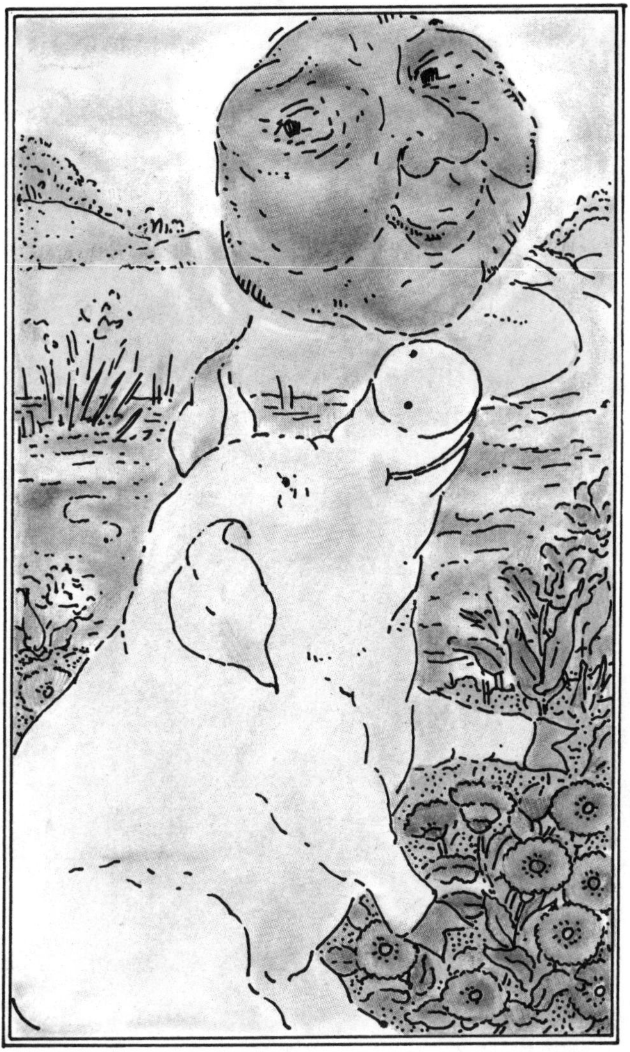

"Oink, oink," said the pig
and swallowed the pancake
in one large gulp.

By then, the woman,

the children,

the farmer,

the goose,

the cat,

the sheep,

and the goat

came running to the brook

where the pig was resting.

"Have you seen a pancake roll by?"

said the woman to the pig.

"Did you make

that wonderful pancake?"

said the pig.

"It was the best I ever ate!"

"You ate our pancake!"

cried the children.

"And we are so hungry!"

"I know what to do,"
  their mother said.
"We shall all go home now.
  And I will make
  an even better pancake
  for everybody."
"A splendid idea," said the pig.
  So the children,
  the farmer,
  the goose,
  the cat,
  the sheep,
  the goat,
  and the pig
  followed the woman home.

There she cooked
the best pancake
she had ever made.
And they ate it
before it could roll away.